Walt Disney's
Snow White
and the Seven Dwarfs

ADAPTED BY NANCY PARENT

This is the story of Snow White, the Seven Dwarfs, a jealous Queen, and a handsome Prince. Read along with me as we embark on an exciting adventure. You will know it is time to turn the page when you hear this sound... Just follow along, and enjoy this wonderful tale about Snow White and all of her friends!

Long ago in a faraway place, there lived a young princess named Snow White. She had hair black as coal, lips red as a rose, and skin white as snow.

Snow White's stepmother, the Queen, was very cruel. Hating anyone more beautiful than she, the Queen treated Snow White like a servant. The princess spent her days scrubbing floors and cooking meals.

Even though Snow White worked very hard, she never complained. Sometimes she dreamed of a handsome prince who would take her away to his castle.

One morning, as Snow White did her chores, a handsome stranger appeared. He found the princess charming, but Snow White was too shy to speak to him.

Inside the castle, the wicked Queen asked her magic mirror, "Magic mirror on the wall, who is the fairest one of all?"

The mirror replied, "You are the fairest." And the Queen was happy for another day.

But as Snow White's beauty grew, the Queen became very jealous. One day, the mirror told her that Snow White was now the fairest in the land.

The Queen called her royal huntsman to the throne room.
"Take Snow White far into the forest and kill her," she
ordered, handing him a carved box. "And bring me back
her heart in this!"

But the huntsman could not harm the princess. He
told Snow White to run away and never come back.

Snow White was so terrified
that she fled into the dark woods.

At last, she came upon a cottage
in a clearing. She went inside and
began to clean.

Meanwhile, the Seven Dwarfs,
who lived in the cottage were on their
way home from a hard day's work in
the diamond mine.

The Dwarfs introduced themselves
as Sleepy, Grumpy, Happy, Doc, Dopey,
Sneezy, and Bashful. And, when they learned
that Snow White could cook, they invited her to stay.
Soon, Snow White came to love the Dwarfs. She felt
safe and happy in their little cottage.

When the wicked Queen learned that Snow White was still alive, she ran to the dungeon. There, she mixed a potion that would change her into an old peddler woman.

Then she took an apple and dipped it into a different potion.

"One taste of this poisoned apple," she cackled, "and Snow White will close her eyes forever!"

Soon, the old woman appeared at Snow White's window. "All alone, my pet?" she asked. "Making pies? It's apple pies that make the menfolk's mouths water."

She held a shiny red apple out to Snow White. "Go on," she urged. "Have a bite."

The birds and the animals of the forest wanted to warn Snow White. They fluttered and flew around the peddler woman, trying to make her drop the apple.

But Snow White came to her rescue and shooed the animals away.

Then she invited the old woman inside.

Suddenly, the Queen came to the edge of a steep cliff. She tried to move a boulder so it would roll down and crush the Dwarfs.

But, at that very moment, lightning struck. The Queen lost her balance and fell to her doom!

The Seven Dwarfs sadly built a glass bed for their beloved Snow White and kept watch over her.

After hearing the story of Snow White, a prince from another
kingdom searched everywhere for her.
He hoped that she was the princess
he had met at the well.

When at last he found her,
the Prince knelt down
and kissed Snow White,
awakening her. Then
they rode off to his
kingdom where
they lived happily
ever after.

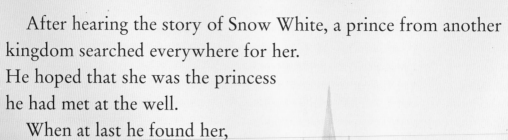